MW00889263

FACT AND FICTION OF AMERICAN COLONIZATION

BY TAMMY GAGNE

CONTENT CONSULTANT
Samuel Fisher, PhD
Assistant Professor of Early American History
The Catholic University of America

Core Library

An Imprint of Abdo Publishing
abdobooks.com

Cover image: The Pilgrims landed in Plymouth, Massachusetts, in 1620.

abdobooks.com

Published by Abdo Publishing, a division of ABDO, PO Box 398166, Minneapolis, Minnesota 55439. Copyright © 2022 by Abdo Consulting Group, Inc. International copyrights reserved in all countries. No part of this book may be reproduced in any form without written permission from the publisher. Core Library™ is a trademark and logo of Abdo Publishing.

Printed in the United States of America, North Mankato, Minnesota
052021
092021

THIS BOOK CONTAINS RECYCLED MATERIALS

Cover Photo: Art Images/Hulton Fine Art Collection/Getty Images
Interior Photos: Rue des Archives/Granger Historical Picture Archive, 4–5; Everett Collection/ Shutterstock Images, 10–11, 18–19, 30, 43, 45; CDC/Science Source, 12; Sarin Images/Granger Historical Picture Archives, 16; Photo Researchers/Science History Images/Alamy, 21; iStockphoto, 25 (beaver), 25 (muskrat), 25 (otter), 25 (background); John Pitcher/iStockphoto, 25 (mink); North Wind Picture Archives, 26–27, 29, 34–35; Red Line Editorial, 37; SeanPavonePhoto/iStockphoto, 38

Editor: Aubrey Zalewski
Series Designer: Ryan Gale

Library of Congress Control Number: 2020948167

Publisher's Cataloging-in-Publication Data

Names: Gagne, Tammy, author.
Title: Fact and fiction of American colonization / by Tammy Gagne
Description: Minneapolis, Minnesota : Abdo Publishing, 2022 | Series: Fact and fiction of American history | Includes online resources and index.
Identifiers: ISBN 9781532195082 (lib. bdg.) | ISBN 9781098215392 (ebook)
Subjects: LCSH: America--Discovery and exploration--Juvenile literature. | Colonization--History--Juvenile literature. | Truthfulness and falsehood--Juvenile literature. | Public opinion--Juvenile literature.
Classification: DDC 973.2--dc23

CONTENTS

DISCOVERING THE AMERICAS

There is a popular account of the Americas' discovery. As the story goes, Europeans in 1492 thought the world was flat. But Italian explorer Christopher Columbus had a theory. He believed that Earth was actually round. He thought he could reach China and India by traveling west instead of east. This would prove the world was round.

In 1486, Columbus approached King Ferdinand and Queen Isabella of Spain. He asked them to fund his journey. They said

Images of Christopher Columbus sometimes show him as a hero.

no at first but eventually agreed. As the story goes, Queen Isabella had to sell some of her jewels to come up with the money. Columbus set sail in August 1492 with three ships. These ships were the *Niña*, *Pinta*, and *Santa María*. By October, he reached land. He was in a new place. He had discovered the Americas.

THE TRUTH ABOUT COLUMBUS

The story of Columbus and his discovery is one of the most famous tales in history. But the popular telling of it is also problematic. Columbus did not discover the Americas. Indigenous peoples had been living there long before Columbus arrived. He also wasn't the first European to visit the Americas. A group of Norse people called the Vikings had made the trip 500 years earlier.

Queen Isabella did not sell her jewels to pay for the voyage. The monarchs borrowed money to pay for it. Columbus even contributed some of his own money. Columbus also wasn't the first person to suggest that the world was round. Many educated Europeans already knew this.

Columbus was also not the hero that many stories make him out to be. On the Caribbean island of Hispaniola, Columbus met the Taino people. They treated him with kindness and generosity. He seized their land for Spain. Many Taino people were killed in this process. Those who survived were forced into slavery. Columbus's arrival was marked by cruelty and terror.

INDIGENOUS PEOPLES' DAY

In 1892, US president Benjamin Harrison established Columbus Day. One hundred years later, the city of Berkeley, California, made a historic change to the holiday. It declared October 12 to be Indigenous Peoples' Day instead. This holiday's purpose is to honor Native Americans. Numerous US cities and states followed Berkeley's lead. By 2019, eight states had adopted the change.

WHY KEEP TELLING THE TALE?

People keep telling this story despite its errors. And it is not the only historical story to mix fiction with facts. Many stories have become unforgettable parts of popular culture. People celebrate the stories in plays and during national holidays, such as Columbus Day and Thanksgiving. Some of these stories cover up darker parts of history. For example, saying Columbus discovered the Americas hides the fact that Columbus led the way for Europeans to take land that was already home to indigenous peoples.

STRAIGHT TO THE
SOURCE

Historian William Fowler spoke about the danger of believing the myths about Christopher Columbus:

> *We've become much more sensitive about indigenous cultures and the harm, the wreckage that the European arrival here in the New World visited upon those people.*
>
> *. . . As we reflect on that and the cost to native peoples here in this world, the damage that was done, I think that sort of mellows the way we might be thinking about Columbus, not suggesting we blame him individually. I don't think that's correct. He was a man of his times. But there was great evil that was done when the Europeans came. Today, perhaps, we think of discovery. We might also think of the word invasion and the result of that. Much good has happened, clearly, but much evil happened, as well.*
>
> Source: "Think You Know the Real Christopher Columbus?" *NPR: Tell Me More*, 10 Oct. 2011, npr.org. Accessed 30 July 2020.

WHAT'S THE BIG IDEA?

Take a close look at this passage. What connections does Fowler make between Columbus and indigenous peoples? How do you think indigenous peoples' history in the Americas might have been different if Columbus had never made his famous voyage?

THE FIRST SETTLERS

Many stories about Columbus end with the explorer landing in a vast wilderness. They describe land that is largely untouched. They show a region inhabited by only a small number of people. Columbus called these people "Indians" in reference to the Indies, another name for the south and southeastern parts of Asia. Columbus thought he had landed in South Asia. Europeans saw Indians as simple people who could benefit from the Europeans' knowledge. These myths lasted throughout the colonization of the Americas.

Christopher Columbus, *right*, did not arrive in an unoccupied land.

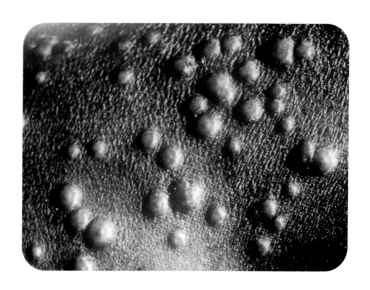

Native Americans died from European diseases such as smallpox. Along with flu-like symptoms, smallpox causes pus-filled blisters to appear on the skin.

THE WILDERNESS MYTH

The Americas were not wilderness when Columbus landed in 1492. In fact, more than 1 million people inhabited North America at the time. From the Penobscot Nation in Maine to the Catawba Nation in South Carolina, many peoples lived in large villages. They had cleared much of the land. Farms dotted the coastline. Farther south, tribes with thousands of members made their homes in Florida and Georgia.

The root of the wilderness myth actually comes from a later time. Thousands of Europeans settled in North America over the next century. As they arrived, they brought diseases. Many indigenous people died from these illnesses. This drove their populations down greatly. With so many dead, the land appeared deserted.

NOT INDIANS

Believing he had made it to the Indies, Columbus called the peoples he encountered, collectively, "Indians." The name stuck in European culture for centuries. But this name was both inaccurate and disrespectful. Each tribe had its own name and culture.

PERSPECTIVES

DIFFERENT WAYS OF LIFE

European settlers often viewed Native Americans as less intelligent. But this was far from the truth. Each tribal nation had its own government. It created laws and drew up treaties with other tribes. In more populated regions, governments managed access to land and water. They had systems for caring for widows and orphans. The indigenous peoples' ways of life were different from the Europeans' ways of doing things. Because of these differences, the Europeans did not consider Native Americans as equal to them.

Even today, many people speak as though there is a single Native American culture. In fact, there are many different Native American cultures still practiced today. The tribal nations at the time of the colonies had complex governments. They were technologically advanced. Their cultures and technologies were just different from those of the Europeans.

Myths may make it easier to think of the Americas as unclaimed land. But the truth was that the New World was only new to those who were not native to it. And those who were native to the land would have it stolen from them for years to come.

THE MYTHS OF POCAHONTAS

One of the most popular stories of American colonization is that of Pocahontas. The tale has been the subject of many books and films. In these accounts, Pocahontas was the daughter of Chief Powhatan, also called Wahunsenacawh. John Smith was an English soldier who claimed he was captured by Powhatan people. According to Smith, Pocahontas saved him when her tribe was about to kill him. She taught him about Powhatan life in what is now Virginia. They formed a relationship. In some versions of the story, the pair fell in love.

It is true that Pocahontas was the daughter of Chief Powhatan. And her tribe did capture Smith. But he was likely not in any danger. After his capture, Smith returned to the Jamestown colony. Pocahontas often visited the colony with members of her tribe. She helped keep peace between the two groups. She was a bright and outgoing young person. What many people get

POCAHONTAS'S NAMES

The name Pocahontas is not entirely accurate. Her most common name was Amonute. People called her Matoaka. Only her father called her by the nickname Pocahontas. This was her late mother's name. It means "playful one." Some historians think that she did not share her real name with John Smith. They say that the Powhatans feared the English could hurt her if they knew it.

Stories and images of John Smith's rescue are likely inaccurate.

wrong is Pocahontas's age. She was around ten years old when she met Smith. Smith was 27.

Years after he met Pocahontas, Smith wrote a book. Smith had fallen on hard times. He did not have much money. Historians argue that Smith might have exaggerated the story to sell more copies. Some even think that he made up the part about the rescue.

The true story of Pocahontas did not end happily. An English navy captain named Samuel Argall took her hostage in 1613. Her captors pressured her to become Christian and change her name to Rebecca. She ended up marrying another Englishman named John Rolfe. After falling ill, she died around the age of 20 in England.

EXPLORE ONLINE

Chapter Two discusses the population of indigenous peoples in the Americas between the 1400s and 1600s. The article below discusses the decline in indigenous populations since Columbus's arrival. As you know, every source is different. How is the information from the article the same as the information in Chapter Two? What new information did you learn from the article?

MASSIVE POPULATION DROP FOUND FOR NATIVE AMERICANS, DNA SHOWS

abdocorelibrary.com/fact-fiction-american-colonization

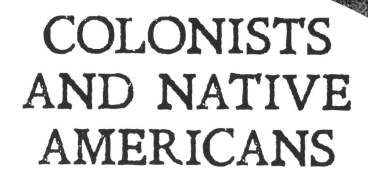

COLONISTS AND NATIVE AMERICANS

When thinking of Thanksgiving, people may recall stories of the Pilgrims. The first group of Pilgrims landed at Plymouth Rock in 1620. This place is in present-day Massachusetts. Shortly after arriving, the Pilgrims came into contact with Native Americans. At first, the European settlers worried that the indigenous people might not be friendly. But the Native Americans welcomed the Pilgrims to the New World.

Historical paintings often depict stereotypes of indigenous people and simplify the relationship between them and the Europeans.

As the story goes, the Pilgrims knew very little about how to live off the new land. The Native Americans shared their knowledge to help the settlers. The Pilgrims were thankful for this guidance. When fall came, they held a feast to show their gratitude. They invited their new neighbors. They spoke different languages and had different customs. But the two groups came together for this celebration of their new friendship.

SOME FIRST THANKSGIVING TRUTHS

The first detail that almost always gets left out of the Thanksgiving retelling is the name of the tribe. It was the Wampanoag people who interacted with the Pilgrims. Most stories cast them simply as Native Americans. This overlooks their existence and unique culture.

The first Thanksgiving was a celebration of the harvest in 1621. There was another reason to celebrate. The English in attendance had just survived a year

A historical painting shows Metacom, a Wampanoag leader, meeting with European settlers. Relations later turned violent as the Europeans took over more tribal land.

of disease and death that took nearly half of the group. Historians are unsure about the circumstances surrounding the Wampanoag's invitation to the feast. Some believe that the Wampanoag leader Massasoit (Ousamequin) came to discuss political matters. Others say that the Wampanoag people might have been in the area visiting other Native tribes, as they did each year after the harvest.

SEEKING ALLIES

Chief Massasoit (Ousamequin) offered the Pilgrims an alliance. The Wampanoag did not get along with the Narragansett. This was another tribe that lived in the region. The Wampanoag wanted the settlers' support. This would make it more difficult for the Narragansett to overpower the Wampanoag. The plan worked. But it also led to other problems. The Wampanoag entered into the agreement in good faith. They did not think the European settlers would dishonor the deal and go to war against them.

Unfortunately, this shared meal did not lead to a peaceful relationship between the Wampanoag people and the European settlers. When the Pilgrims first arrived, Massasoit wanted an alliance with them. He thought this would help his people. But over the next 50 years, Europeans took more and more land and resources from the Wampanoag. At one point they even went to war.

THE SALE OF MANHATTAN

Many people tell the story about the sale of Manhattan. This myth even appears in certain textbooks. The Dutch purchased the New York island from the Lenape people in 1626. The myth claims that they bought it for just $24 worth of beads and trinkets. In the 1600s, $24 was equal to approximately $1,500 today. If the story were true, the purchase would be one of the biggest bargains in history. The land was worth a lot to the Dutch because it was on the Hudson River. The land gave easy access to fur-trapping territories in the north.

A letter to Dutch officials provides some proof that a deal took place. But it does not state what the Lenape received in return. Additionally, it is likely that the deal involved goods such as clothing, muskets, and tools, not just beads and trinkets. The retelling of this myth suggests that the Lenape people were gullible. It shows the Lenape as selling valuable land for something worthless.

STORIES TOLD THROUGH SONG

In 2014, the concert opera *Purchase of Manhattan* was performed in New York City. Money from the concert went toward creating the Lenape Center in Manhattan. The Lenape Center celebrates the community, culture, and arts of the Lenape people. Brent Michael Davids composed the piece. He put a new spin on the often-told tale. His opera tells the story from the perspective of the Lenape people. It shows how the Dutch took advantage of them. As a Mohican, Davids is passionate about accurate retellings of Native American history.

Another problem with the story has to do with a cultural difference. Buying land was a common practice in Dutch society. But the Lenape viewed land as something that could not be owned. This view was held by many Native American peoples. It is unlikely that the tribe was agreeing to sell the land to the Dutch settlers. They may have meant only to let the Dutch use the land.

FUR TRAPPING IN
NEW YORK

Several animal species made their homes along the Hudson River in New York in the 1600s. Beavers, otters, muskrats, and minks were all used in the fur trade. The Dutch traded with Native Americans for furs, especially beaver furs. How does knowing this help you understand how valuable Manhattan was?

MINK

MUSKRAT

OTTER

BEAVER

RELIGIOUS FREEDOM

The US Constitution provides Americans freedom of religion. This freedom is often thought to go even further back than this governing document. Stories about the Pilgrims sailing to North America for religious freedom are common. Everyone could live and worship as they wished in the New World. It is part of why other groups made the voyage. One example is the Puritans. Puritans were a group of Christians who thought the Church of England needed to change. In England, they were sometimes persecuted for their beliefs.

The first British settlements were founded on Christian beliefs.

They left so they could practice their religion the way they wanted.

NOT TRUE FREEDOM

Tales of religious freedom in colonial America are largely myths. Early settlers did practice different religions. But most did not tolerate other religions well. European settlers often labeled Native Americans as heathens. The settlers did this because the indigenous people did not practice Christianity.

Religion in the colonies was more diverse than in European countries. However, this diversity often led to conflict. Some colonies did allow people to practice different forms of Christianity. Pennsylvania was one of these. But many settlers in other colonies didn't tolerate other European religions. Puritans in New England banned non-Puritans from living in their colonies. In the worst situations, religion was used as an excuse to kill people. Quakers are a group of Christians. They believe

Puritans executed Quakers in Massachusetts during the 1600s.

Puritans in Salem, Massachusetts, accused one another of being witches.

in having personal connections to God without church leaders. Between 1659 and 1661, four Quakers were banned from Boston, Massachusetts, because of their religion. But they returned to the city. They were all hanged as a result.

People of different faiths who were not banned were persecuted. Early colonial governments banned

Jews and Catholics from serving in public office. Catholics could not own property or vote.

WITCH TRIALS

Many people know the story of the Salem witch trials. Several young girls in Salem, Massachusetts, began acting strangely in 1691. For no clear reason, they would scream, make odd sounds, and throw things. Their parents assumed that someone must have cast spells on them. They urged their daughters to name who had done this to them. The girls

PERSPECTIVES
A MEDICAL EXPLANATION?

Some mental health experts think that the trouble in Salem came from a medical problem. They think that a fungus called ergot caused the accusers to hallucinate. Ergot is found in rye, wheat, and other types of edible grasses. People commonly ate these at the time. However, others disagree with this theory. They point out that the accusers' family members ate the same food. The rest of the family members did not have these problems. The accusers also did not suffer from any of the other effects of ergot poisoning.

accused several women of witchcraft. This crime was punishable by death in Puritan societies. Some stories say the accused witches were burned at the stake.

This tale mixes fact with fiction. People did accuse others of witchcraft in Salem during the 1690s. The young girls claimed that the witches' spirits visited them. This kind of evidence was taken only on people's word. There was no real proof of wrongdoing. Often those who were called witches were those who were disliked. Some were targeted because they were of a lower class.

In all, 20 people were put to death during the Salem witch trials in 1692 and 1693. But they were not actually burned at the stake.

GETTING REVENGE

Shortly after the first witchcraft accusations, even more people came forward. One of them was a girl named Ann Putnam Jr. Her mother, her cousin, and the family's servant also accused dozens of people of witchcraft. Many of the accused were enemies of the Putnam family.

Most of them were hanged. Six of the people who were killed were not women. These men disagreed with the witch trials. Later they were accused of witchcraft. Five were hanged. One man was crushed with stones while being forced to admit his guilt. The trials were fueled by a belief that the accused did not follow God. And those who did not follow God were called witches. The people of Salem used this belief to target others in the community.

FURTHER EVIDENCE

Chapter Four discusses what actually happened during the Salem witch trials. What was one of the main points of this chapter? What evidence is included to support this point? Read the article at the website below. Does the information in the article support the main point of the chapter? Does it present new evidence?

THE SALEM WITCH TRIALS

abdocorelibrary.com/fact-fiction-american-colonization

THE
COLONIES

During the colonial period, the land near the East Coast was divided into 13 colonies. These colonies were Connecticut, Delaware, Georgia, Maryland, Massachusetts, New Hampshire, New Jersey, New York, North Carolina, Pennsylvania, Rhode Island, South Carolina, and Virginia. These settlements belonged to Great Britain in the 1700s.

American history is filled with stories about the 13 colonies. They are where the United States was born. However, for most of the period, there were really only 12 colonies,

William Penn, *center*, tried to unite the colonists in Pennsylvania and Delaware.

not 13. Delaware was not originally a colony. It was part of New York until 1682. Then it became part of Pennsylvania. William Penn founded the colony of Pennsylvania. He wanted the bay area to become part of his colony. Adding the land gave Pennsylvania access to the ocean. But those in Delaware and those in Pennsylvania did not get along. So Delaware had its own government. Delaware separated from Pennsylvania in 1776. Many people still talk about the 13 colonies because Delaware eventually became its own colony.

THE FIRST STATE

Although Delaware was not originally a colony, it was an important part of US history. It had an honor that none of the 12 colonies could claim. Delaware became the first American settlement to ratify itself as a state following the American Revolution (1775–1783). The historic event took place on December 7, 1787.

SPEAKING ENGLISH

A popular myth is that English was the most common language in the

THE COLONIES
IN 1775

The map below shows American colonies in 1775. The boundaries changed many times. Because Delaware became its own colony, it is often shown as a colony on maps before 1776. In 1763, Great Britain reserved land for Native nations. What do you notice about how the land was divided?

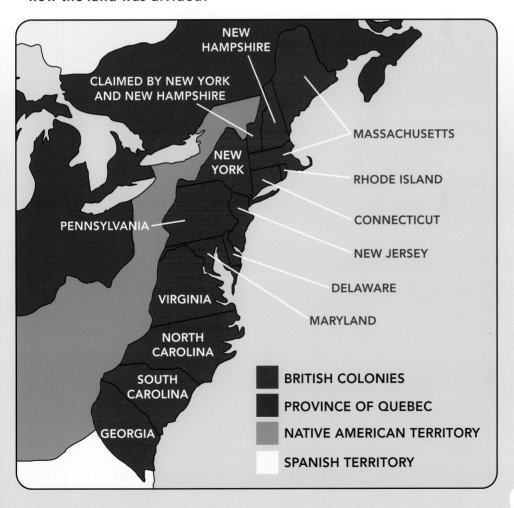

NEW HAMPSHIRE

CLAIMED BY NEW YORK AND NEW HAMPSHIRE

MASSACHUSETTS

NEW YORK

RHODE ISLAND

CONNECTICUT

PENNSYLVANIA

NEW JERSEY

DELAWARE

VIRGINIA

MARYLAND

NORTH CAROLINA

SOUTH CAROLINA

GEORGIA

BRITISH COLONIES

PROVINCE OF QUEBEC

NATIVE AMERICAN TERRITORY

SPANISH TERRITORY

Spanish influences can still be seen in buildings in Saint Augustine, Florida.

North American colonies. After all, Great Britain founded many of them. People from Great Britain spoke English.

The truth is that colonists spoke many languages. Each European country that colonized North America brought its own language. Great Britain was not the only or the first nation to set up colonies in North America. Spain had settled on the North American continent long before the British. One of the first Spanish settlements in North America was founded in Saint Augustine, Florida, in 1565. Spanish-speaking people already lived in parts of Florida and New Mexico when the British founded Jamestown in Virginia in 1607. In 1624, the Dutch settled in the New York area. And in the 1700s, thousands of Germans settled in Pennsylvania. These are just a few examples. English was a popular language in the American colonies. But it was far from the only one spoken.

Native languages were among the most spoken in North America in the colonial era. In 1492, indigenous peoples spoke more than 300 different languages in the area that is now the United States. Today, around 175 of those languages still exist. The rest have been lost due to population loss and forced assimilation. During the 1800s and 1900s, the US government made Native American children attend boarding schools. They were

NATIVE LANGUAGES

The English that the colonists spoke was not the same English spoken by people living in Great Britain. Many of the words were the same. But the colonists developed an American accent. They also added words to the English language from Native American languages. For example, the word *chipmunk* came from the Algonquin word *chitmunk*. The word *potato* can be traced to the Taino word *batata*. Many place names in the colonies came from Native American words. *Massachusetts*, for instance, was a Wampanoag word meaning "by the hills."

not allowed to speak their tribal languages or practice their cultural traditions.

Knowing the truth behind the stories from the colonial era begins with separating the myths from the facts. Repeating some of these stories may seem harmless. But many of them include fiction that contributes to the spread of discrimination. Knowing the truth can help stop this spread.

STRAIGHT TO THE
SOURCE

Phillip M. Carter is a foreign language expert. He explains how Spanish came to the United States:

News stories have recently raised the misconception that native Spanish speakers are only now beginning to populate areas of the United States en masse. Although recent Census reports show that the US Hispanic population has experienced an upsurge since the early 1990s, Hispanic communities and varieties of the Spanish language have been maintained in the United States for well more than four centuries. In fact, Spanish actually antedates English in the areas that now make up the composite United States—a fact that surprises many Americans. In terms of continuity and longevity in the United States, the Spanish language is second only to Native American languages that were spoken for centuries prior to colonization.

Source: "Do You Speak American? Spanish in the US." *PBS*, n.d., pbs.org. Accessed 30 July 2020.

CONSIDER YOUR AUDIENCE

Adapt this passage for a different audience, such as your friends. Write a blog post conveying this same information for the new audience. How does your post differ from the original text and why?

IMPORTANT DATES

1492
Christopher Columbus sails west and arrives in the Caribbean. Eventually, people credit him as the discoverer of the Americas, though indigenous peoples had already been living there.

1565
One of the first Spanish settlements in North America is founded in Saint Augustine, Florida.

1607
English settlers found the colony of Jamestown in Virginia.

1613
Pocahontas is taken hostage by Samuel Argall. In the following years, she is pressured to change her name and become Christian.

1621

The Pilgrims celebrate the harvest, which later becomes known as the first Thanksgiving. But the celebration is not the start of a peaceful relationship between the Pilgrims and the Wampanoag people.

1626

The Dutch purchase Manhattan from the Lenape people, likely in exchange for goods such as clothing, muskets, and tools.

1692

The Salem witch trials begin in Massachusetts. These target disliked people in the community.

1776

Delaware separates from Pennsylvania, becoming the thirteenth colony.

STOP AND ★THINK

Surprise Me

This book discusses some of the key events that happened in American colonies. After reading this book, what two or three facts about American colonization did you find most surprising? Write a few sentences about each fact. Why did you find each fact surprising?

Say What?

Studying American history can mean learning a lot of new vocabulary. Find five words in this book you've never seen before. Use a dictionary to find out what they mean. Then write the meanings in your own words and use each word in a new sentence.

Dig Deeper

After reading this book, what questions do you still have about American colonization? With an adult's help, find a few reliable sources that can help you answer your questions. Write a paragraph about what you learned.

Another View

This book talks about the facts and fiction of American colonization. As you know, every source is different. Ask an adult to help you find another source about American colonization. Write a short essay comparing and contrasting the new source's point of view with that of this book's author. What is the point of view of each source? How are they similar and why? How are they different and why?

GLOSSARY

alliance
an agreement between
groups to work together

antedate
to come before in time

assimilation
the process of becoming
part of a group's culture

culture
shared traditions and values
within a certain group

discrimination
the unjust treatment of a
group of people based
on their race, gender, or
other characteristics

en masse
as a whole

gullible
easily fooled

hallucinate
to see or hear something
that is not truly present

heathen
a negative name for a person
who does not believe in the
god of the Christian Bible

ratify
to officially approve
an agreement or
governing document

ONLINE RESOURCES

To learn more about the facts and fiction of American colonization, visit our free resource websites below.

Visit **abdocorelibrary.com** or scan this QR code for free Common Core resources for teachers and students, including vetted activities, multimedia, and booklinks, for deeper subject comprehension.

Visit **abdobooklinks.com** or scan this QR code for free additional online weblinks for further learning. These links are routinely monitored and updated to provide the most current information available.

LEARN MORE

Gagne, Tammy. *Fact and Fiction of the American Revolution.* Abdo Publishing, 2022.

Medina, Nico. *Who Was Leif Erikson?* Penguin Workshop, 2018.

INDEX

About the Author

Tammy Gagne has written dozens of books for both adults and children. Her recent titles include *Fact and Fiction of American Invention* and *Fact and Fiction of the American Revolution*. She lives in northern New England with her husband, her son, and a menagerie of pets.